For all the Jills and Pablos everywhere.
Because the world is much more fun with them in it.

Margarita del Mazo

For Frida, who never stops making me happy.

José Fragoso

Princess Jill Never Sits Still
Somos8 Series

© Text: Margarita del Mazo, 2019
© Illustrations: José Fragoso, 2019
© Edition: NubeOcho, 2020
© Translation: Ben Dawlatly, 2020
www.nubeocho.com · hello@nubeocho.com

Original title: *La princesa Sara no para*
Text editing: Rebecca Packard and Cecilia Ross

First edition: April 2020
ISBN: 978-84-17123-83-3
Legal deposit: M-19646-2019

Printed in China respecting
international labor standards.

Princess Jill never sits still

margarita del mazo
josé fragoso

nubeOCHO

In a peaceful kingdom, where time trickled by without haste,
a princess called Jill was born.

The queen and king were happy. They had always wanted a little girl whose hair they could put in ringlets and whom they could clothe in exquisite dresses.

Jill was very curious, and she
soon learned to crawl.

The gardener then began to wail,
"Your Highness! Princess Jill never sits still!"

In the evenings, when it was time to go to bed, little Jill would stay up for hours.

Then the nanny started to complain, "Your Majesty! Princess Jill never sits still!"

At lunch, she'd have more fun with the food than anybody else.

Then the butlers protested, "Your Royal Highness! Princess Jill never sits still!"

The princess's favorite place in the castle was the kitchen. That's where she discovered music.

Then the cook whined, "Your Royal Highness! Princess Jill never sits still!"

One day, the monarchs realized that the princess had never sat on her throne.
She would jump on it, run around it, and climb on top of it. But not once had she sat on it.

"Goodness gracious! This is a tragedy!" they gasped. The queen and king
decided to look for some help right away.

The greatest wise men in the land came to study little Jill,
and in the end they all came to the same conclusion.

"Your Majesties, the princess has the *dancing beat* in both her feet. The only cure is
to wear these iron boots for a month," counseled the wise man with the longest beard.

With her new boots, Jill was more or less calm during the day. But when her feet were freed at bedtime, the princess ran off, and all through the night, there was no way of catching her.

The next day, the queen and king filled the kingdom with witches and sorcerers from all over the world. Enchantments and spells could be heard echoing through all the palace hallways.

"Your Highnesses, Princess Jill has a case of *I-can't-keep-my-bottom-still*. She needs a spoonful of this potion at dinnertime," the smelliest, grubbiest witch assured them.

But the queen and king quickly realized that the witch's concoction didn't work either. They were beside themselves with worry when they finally went to bed that night. But what they didn't know was that the worst was yet to come.

The following morning a letter was delivered to the palace; it was from
the monarchs of Farawaylandia, announcing they would be visiting. Their son,
Prince Pablo, wished to make the acquaintance of princesses and princes from
other kingdoms.

"How are we ever going to properly introduce the two if the princess is never sitting on her throne?" lamented the queen.

When the Farawaylandian royal family arrived, the queen and king were waiting for them in the grand hall.

A band with trumpets and drums announced their arrival. Behind them, a jester was doing somersaults and making funny faces, bringing joy and laughter to all the members of the royal court.

"We are eager to meet the princess. Where is she?" asked the illustrious father of Prince Pablo.

"She's up there," replied the queen nervously.

"In her bedchamber?"

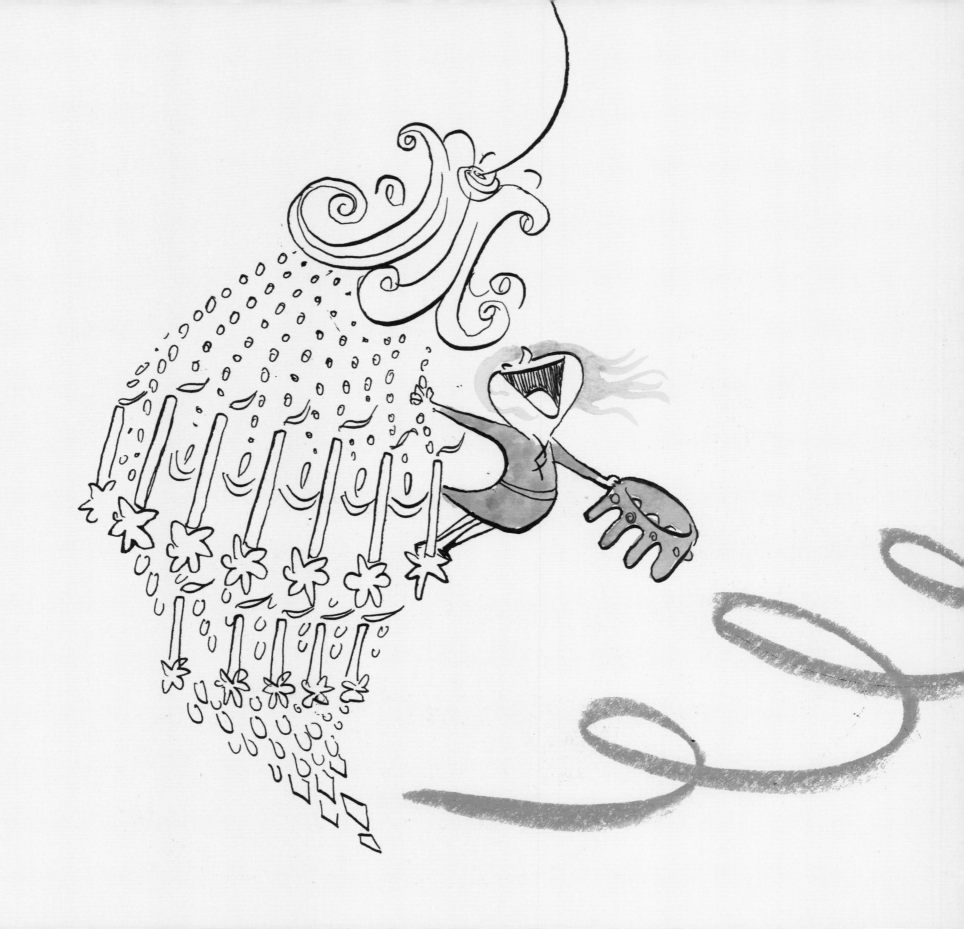

"No," sighed the queen. "She's on the chandelier!"

"Bravo! The princess is an acrobat!" Prince Pablo's parents applauded.

They were right! Until that moment, the queen and king had never realized their daughter was an acrobat. The queen, swelling with pride, asked,

"And Prince Pablo? Has he not come?"

"Why yes, he has, my dear. He's up there, too!" replied the queen and king of Farawaylandia.